Dear Parents:

Congratulations! Your child is taking the first steps on an exciting journey. The destination? Independent reading!

STEP INTO READING® will help your child get there. The program offers five steps to reading success. Each step includes fun stories and colorful art or photographs. In addition to original fiction and books with favorite characters, there are Step into Reading Non-Fiction Readers, Phonics Readers and Boxed Sets, Sticker Readers, and Comic Readers—a complete literacy program with something to interest every child.

Learning to Read, Step by Step!

Ready to Read Preschool–Kindergarten
• big type and easy words • rhyme and rhythm • picture clues
For children who know the alphabet and are eager to begin reading.

Reading with Help Preschool–Grade 1
• basic vocabulary • short sentences • simple stories
For children who recognize familiar words and sound out new words with help.

Reading on Your Own Grades 1–3
• engaging characters • easy-to-follow plots • popular topics
For children who are ready to read on their own.

Reading Paragraphs Grades 2–3
• challenging vocabulary • short paragraphs • exciting stories
For newly independent readers who read simple sentences with confidence.

Ready for Chapters Grades 2–4
• chapters • longer paragraphs • full-color art
For children who want to take the plunge into chapter books but still like colorful pictures.

STEP INTO READING® is designed to give every child a successful reading experience. The grade levels are only guides; children will progress through the steps at their own speed, developing confidence in their reading.

Remember, a lifetime love of reading starts with a single step!

Copyright © 2021 Warner Bros. Entertainment Inc.
SPACE JAM: A NEW LEGACY and all related characters
and elements © and ™ Warner Bros. Entertainment Inc. (s21)

Step into Reading, Random House, and the Random House colophon are registered trademarks of
Penguin Random House LLC.

Visit us on the Web!
StepIntoReading.com
rhcbooks.com

Educators and librarians, for a variety of teaching tools, visit us at RHTeachersLibrarians.com

ISBN 978-0-593-38230-1 (trade) — ISBN 978-0-593-38231-8 (lib. bdg.)
ISBN 978-0-593-38232-5 (ebook)

Printed in the United States of America

10 9 8 7 6 5 4 3 2

by Daniel Hayes

illustrated by Red Central Ltd

Random House 🏠 New York

LeBron James is the
best basketball player.
He is strong, fast,
and has all the moves!

LeBron has a big game
against the Goon Squad.
Who will be on his team?

"What's up, doc?" says Bugs Bunny.

"I need your help,"

LeBron says.

To round up a team for LeBron,

Bugs needs a vehicle.

He borrows

Marvin the Martian's spaceship.

"You have made me very angry,"

Marvin says.

LeBron and Bugs

fly to a big city.

They want Super Heroes

on their team.

LeBron does not like

being the sidekick.

They find Daffy Duck
and Porky Pig.
Daffy has become . . .
Super Duck!

He will join the team

if he can be the coach.

It is a deal!

The next stop

is a desert world.

They find Bugs's old friends

Wile E. Coyote and Road Runner.

They will add

speed to the team.

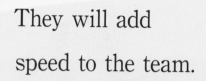

Next, Bugs finds

Sylvester the cat and Tweety.

They can join the team

if Sylvester promises

to stop chasing Tweety.

"Can we get some players

who know how to play basketball?"

LeBron asks.

Elmer Fudd has
chased Bugs for years,
but he wants to help
win the game.

Bugs thinks Yosemite Sam
will give the team energy.
"You have a deal, varmint!"
shouts Sam.

The next player
finds Daffy and Bugs!

Taz jumps

onto the window.

of the spaceship.

Bugs likes his energy.

The team needs
a veteran player.
Granny has that covered.

Speedy Gonzales
is tough and fast!
The team is
almost complete.

Bugs finds

Lola Bunny on the world

of the Amazons.

"We cannot win without you,"

he says.

Lola knows she has to help

her Looney Tunes friends.

The team is coming together.

LeBron thinks that
with a little training,
they can be good.

Gossamer and Foghorn Leghorn join, adding some size!

In their uniforms, the Tune Squad
is looking like a real team.

It is game time.

The Goon Squad looks fierce,

and they are eager to play!

LeBron, Bugs, and
the rest of their team
are ready to win!

SPACE JAM: A NEW LEGACY and all related characters and elements © and ™ Warner Bros. Entertainment Inc. (s21)